Snip, Snip, Little Lambs

Snip, Snip, Little Lambs

Written and illustrated by

Tomie dePaola

WHISTLESTOP®

Troll

Winter was finally over at Fiddle-Dee-Dee Farms. The snow had melted, and it was beginning to get warm outside. The Woolsey children couldn't wait to run and jump and play in the fields again.

"As soon as the mud dries up," said Mama.

"When will that be?" asked Mary and Tom and Tim.

"It won't be long," said Papa.

Each day it was sunnier and a little warmer. Each day, they looked for the spring flowers to poke their heads up in the garden. And each day, Mary and Tom and Tim made plans to build a kite to fly from the top of the hill.

Then one day Papa said, "The sun is shining. The mud's all gone, and now you can play outside." "Hooray!" shouted Mary and Tom and Tim.

"But first it's time for spring haircuts," Papa told them.

All winter long, the Woolseys' fleece had grown thick and curly.

It kept them nice and warm in the snow, but in spring, everybody in the Woolsey family got haircuts.

Clip, clip, clip.
Clip, clip, clip.
Clip, clip, clip.

Spring was such a wonderful time of the year.

But that very night, a cold wind blew down from the north country.

"Wooo," the wind howled, as it rushed around the house.

Papa Woolsey made a big fire in the fireplace.
Mama Woolsey made a fire in the kitchen stove.

Granny Woolsey piled quilts on everyone's bed.
Mary and Tom and Tim shivered and huddled in
front of the fire. It was soooo cold.

As the fires died down, everyone went to bed

...except Granny.

"Well, this is a surprise!" said Papa Woolsey when they woke up the next morning and looked out. Fiddle-Dee-Dee Farms was white with snow.

"It's too cold to go out today," said Mama.
"Especially with your haircuts," said Papa.
"Oh, no," cried the Woolsey children. "Just when we could play outside again."

"I wish we hadn't gotten those haircuts," said Mary.

"Now we can't have any fun," said Tom and Tim.

"Oh, yes, you can!" said Granny. "I've been busy all night."

And Mary and Tom and Tim had a grand time outside, wearing their haircuts, which Granny had made into brand-new sweaters!

Published by WhistleStop, an imprint & registered
trademark of Troll Communications L.L.C.
Text and illustrations copyright © 1989 by Tomie dePaola.
All rights reserved. Published simultaneously in Canada.

Reprinted by arrangement with G.P. Putnam's Sons.

Printed in U.S.A.

10 9 8 7 6 5 4 3 2 1